DISNEY · PIXAR

# WALL·E

### ADAPTED BY
Annie Auerbach

### ILLUSTRATED BY
the Disney Storybook Artists

DISNEP
PRESS

New York

In the twenty-ninth century, the Earth was covered in trash. There was so much of it that plants couldn't even grow. All the humans had gone to live in space long ago.

A small, dusty robot named WALL·E and his pet cockroach were the only ones left. It was WALL·E's job to clean up the trash and stack it neatly.

WALL·E had been there for hundreds of years. He didn't know if he would ever be done. He wished he had a friend.

One day, a robot named EVE landed on Earth. WALL•E liked her right away. He rescued her from a sandstorm and brought her back to his trailer, where he showed her the treasures he had found while cleaning up the trash.

Then he played a video of a musical. WALL•E knew the songs by heart. He pretended a hubcap was a hat and danced to the music. EVE giggled. She had never met anyone like WALL•E.

When the song was over, WALL•E remembered something he had just found that he wanted to show EVE: a plant. As soon as she saw it, her front panel opened and a beam of light locked on to the plant and moved it toward her. Once EVE had the plant, she shut down.

"Eee-vah?" asked WALL•E. But she didn't reply. "Eee-vah!!!" he cried. No matter what he tried, she never opened her eyes or said anything.

Before long, EVE's spaceship came back for her. It turned out that she had been sent to Earth to search for plant life.

WALL·E didn't know this. He just wanted to be with his new friend. As the spaceship took off, he grabbed on to the outside and held on tightly as it roared through space.

*"Eee-vah!"* he called out. But it was no use. She was still shut down.

Soon the spaceship reached the *Axiom*, the huge star
liner that was home to the humans. EVE was activated and
gave the Captain the plant. If the plant was identified by the
ship's holo-detector, then that would mean the Earth had been
cleaned up enough for the humans to go back.

The Captain was very excited. But a robot named
Autopilot was not. He ordered another robot to steal the plant.

Luckily, EVE and WALL•E found the plant before it
was too late.

As EVE and WALL•E
raced back toward the holo-detector
with the plant, Auto took over. He ordered
the *Axiom*'s stewards to find WALL•E and EVE.
    But WALL•E and EVE were not alone. WALL•E had made
friends with a group of malfunctioning robots. When the
stewards were about to capture WALL•E and EVE, WALL•E's new
friends fought them off. The two robots escaped!

WALL•E and EVE finally made it to the holo-detector. Auto tried to shut it down. WALL•E raced over to keep the holo-detector from closing, but he began to lose power.

Finally, the Captain was able to turn off Auto. The plant was identified, and the *Axiom* headed toward Earth. By that time, WALL•E wasn't doing so well.

As soon as the *Axiom* landed, EVE did her best to fix WALL•E, using parts from his trailer.

Before long, WALL•E was working properly.

The humans had begun to look around Earth and were hopeful about their new lives there. Everyone was very happy.

No one was happier than WALL•E, though. He finally had a true friend.